To every child who knows the excitement of a pair of new (or not-so-new) skates — BO

To Kyle, who pushes me to be the best version of myself, but still loves the version that I am — KK

For my dad, Bobby's (and my!) biggest fan — JP

Text copyright © 2020 by Bobby Orr and Kara Kootstra | Illustrations copyright © 2020 by Jennifer Phelan

Tundra Books, an imprint of Penguin Random House Canada Young Readers, a division of Penguin Random House of Canada Limited

Library and Archives Canada Cataloguing in Publication

Title: Bobby Orr and the hand-me-down skates / written by Bobby Orr and Kara Kootstra ; illustrated by Jennifer Phelan.
Names: Orr, Bobby, 1948- author. | Kootstra, Kara, author. | Phelan, Jennifer, illustrator.
Identifiers: Canadiana (print) 20190222328 | Canadiana (ebook) 20190222336 | ISBN 9780735265325 (hardcover) | ISBN 9780735265332 (EPUB)
Subjects: LCSH: Orr, Bobby, 1948-—Juvenile fiction.
Classification: LCC PS8629.O72 B63 2020 | DDC jC813/.6—dc23

Issued in print and electronic formats.

Published simultaneously in the United States by Tundra Books of Northern New York,
an imprint of Penguin Random House Canada Young Readers, a division of Penguin Random House of Canada Limited

Library of Congress Control Number: 2019954100

Edited by Samantha Swenson
Designed by John Martz
The art in this book was rendered in oil pastel and watercolor pencil.
The text was set in Palatino Sans.

Printed and bound in China

www.penguinrandomhouse.ca

1 2 3 4 5   24 23 22 21 20

Penguin Random House
tundra | TUNDRA BOOKS

BOBBY ORR

AND THE HAND-ME-DOWN SKATES

Bobby Orr and Kara Kootstra · illustrated by Jennifer Phelan

tundra

BOBBY lived in a small town by a big lake.

He loved to fish.

He loved to play baseball.

But more than anything else, Bobby loved the game of HOCKEY.

He played hockey at the school rink before his morning classes. He played hockey after school with his friends on the frozen lake. He even played hockey in his dreams.

So of course, when Bobby's eleventh birthday was just around the corner, there was only one thing on his wish list:

A new pair of skates.

He had seen the exact pair he wanted in the window of the
sports shop in town. They were made of smooth, black leather.
The blades were an untouched, gleaming silver. And the bright
white laces were tied into perfect bows.

Bobby could picture himself gliding across the ice and scoring
a game-winning goal in his beautiful new skates.

Leading up to his birthday, Bobby left all kinds of hints for his parents about the new skates.

He left a flyer with a picture of the skates on top of his father's newspaper.

He pointed them out to his mother whenever they passed the sports shop.

He even made a big production about how tight his old skates were.

On the morning of his eleventh birthday, when his parents gave him a big box with a shiny blue bow on top, Bobby was sure his new skates were inside. He untied the ribbon, ripped off the paper, opened the top and took out his brand-new . . .

. . . Hand-Me-Down skates.

"Your brother outgrew these at the end of last season, so I took them in to get sharpened and put in some new laces. They almost look new, don't they?" his father asked.

The skates did not look anything like the skates in the shop window.

HAND-ME-DOWN SKATES

SCUFFED, BROWN LEATHER

BROTHER FEET SMELL

Fig. 1

RUST PATCHES

FROM-THE-STORE SKATES

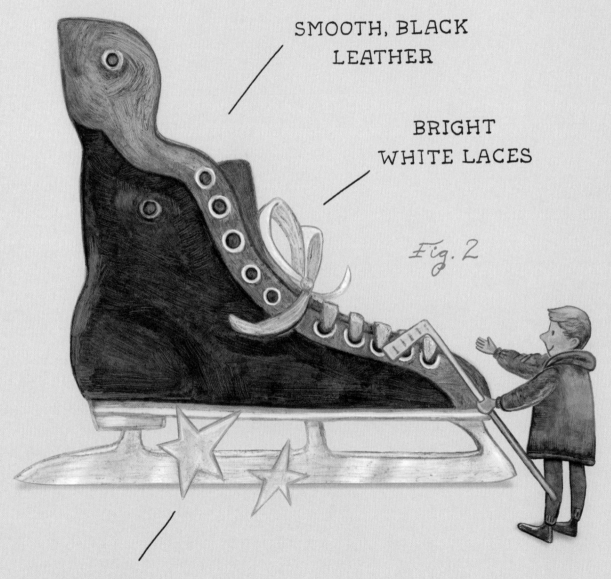

SMOOTH, BLACK
LEATHER

BRIGHT
WHITE LACES

Fig. 2

SPARKLES

Bobby smiled, trying to hide his disappointment.

"Go ahead and try them on, Bobby," said his mother.

Bobby put the skates on. They were at least one size too big, and he couldn't imagine himself staying upright in these skates, let alone scoring a game-winning goal.

His father pushed on the toes of the skates. "You'll grow into them, sport. But in the meantime . . ." Bobby's father crumpled a sheet of newspaper and stuck it into the toes of the skates. When Bobby put them back on, they didn't fit him perfectly, but they did feel a lot better.

"Thanks, Mom and Dad. I can't wait to try them out," he said.

It wasn't easy adjusting to his "new" Hand-Me-Down skates at hockey practice.

In the first drill, he tripped and fell backwards onto the ice.

During his second drill, a speed skating exercise,
Bobby knocked down every single pylon.

And his third drill was the worst — he collided with a teammate, sending him headfirst into the boards!

Bobby was feeling very frustrated, not to mention extremely sore. But by the next drill, the skates were starting to feel more comfortable, and by the end of the practice, he was sailing up the ice in his Hand-Me-Down skates as though they were extensions of his very own feet.

From that moment on, the Hand-Me-Down skates accompanied Bobby all over town. In the early winter mornings, when the sun had just begun to wash over the darkened sky, the skates hung over his shoulders as he walked to the ice rink for his before-school practice.

Bobby would lace up his Hand-Me-Down skates and join in a neighborhood game of shinny with his friends. Setting up a couple of boots or sticks to mark the net posts, they would play until it was too dark to see the puck in front of them, their faces red from the cold.

SEC. ROW SEAT

28 E 38

SOUTH MEZZANINE

WED. JAN. 17

Maple Leaf Gardens
LIMITED

NATIONAL HOCKEY LEAGUE
TORONTO MAPLE LEAFS

Bobby's Hand-Me-Down skates were even with him when his dream of playing at Maple Leaf Gardens came true! His team was invited to play a game before seeing the Toronto Maple Leafs in action. After their match was over, Bobby cheered for his Leafs and his favorite players, Tim Horton and George Armstrong, the Hand-Me-Down skates by his side.

A few weeks before his twelfth birthday, Bobby's father gave him some exciting news.

"A friend of mine has watched you playing and sees how much you love the game," he said. "He's offered to buy you a brand-new pair of skates! What do you say we go into town tomorrow and pick them out?"

Bobby could barely contain his excitement! He was going to get his dream skates! He fell asleep that night imagining himself in the shiny black skates from the window.

The next morning, Bobby and his father went into town to pick up his new skates. The owner of the sports store measured Bobby's feet and gave him lots of different skates to try on. At last, he brought out the black skates that Bobby had seen in the window, and when Bobby put them on, they felt as though they had been made just for him.

"I think we have a winner," Bobby's father said with a smile.

Bobby took his new skates out of the box as soon as he got home, anxious to go down to the lake and try them out. As he reached for his stick, he noticed the Hand-Me-Down skates hanging in his closet and paused.

The skates weren't new or shiny. They hadn't felt like they were made just for him. And yet, as Bobby looked up at them, he felt a twinge of sadness. They had been with him for some very special moments, and Bobby realized that made the Hand-Me-Down skates pretty special too.

Bobby had an idea. He picked up the skates and walked down the hallway to his little brother's room.

He presented the Hand-Me-Down skates to his brother and watched as his face lit up with excitement.

Bobby felt his sadness fade. The skates had found their place, and Bobby hoped his brother would have as many special moments with them as he had.

And he did.